VICTOR
THE HERO
WHALE

A story about a Hero Whale called Victor and his fight against ocean plastics and unsustainable fishing.

In support of

UOCEAN®
2050

Victor the whale was a happy chap,
He loved nothing more than a long swim lap.

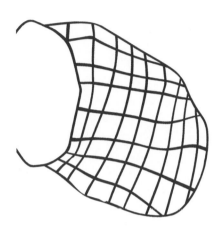

But one day, as he was swimming out in a bay,
He got caught in some plastic, he said
"Oh No Way!"

Victor struggled and thrashed every where,
But the more he moved, he entangled in
despair.

Victor called out for help, but no one was near,
Where are my friends to help me get clear?

As the night drew close and the sun began to set,
Victor grew tired, weary and upset.

He had been stuck in the net for hours on end,
And he was starting to lose hope, his only best
friend.

But just when things were looking so bleak,
A boat in the horizon, appeared so unique.

It was a trawling fishing boat, with a kind and gentle crew.
Who were out on the water, just like me and you.

The fishermen saw Victor and came to a halt!
The net they had lost, they knew it was their
fault.

Working hard through the night,
to cut the plastic free, By the morning sun,
Victor was back in the deep blue sea!

He was so very grateful and no longer sad.
He thanked the fishermen, forgave them and
was glad.

He vowed to return the favour, on any given day,
If they kept the ocean clean and nets out of the bay.

Months went by and he swam a 1000 miles,
But he never forgot that troublesome trial.

He thought of them often, and how he got caught,
Why was the net left, without a second thought?

One stormy night, as the winds began to howl,
The fishermen's boat, got into a scowl.

It was tossed around by the tall angry waves,
The fishermen were scared, and were left in a daze.

Just when things were starting to look grim,
Victor appeared, they shouted "Yes yes, it is
him!"

He used his mighty tail, to push the boat ashore,
And the fishermen were grateful and safe once more.

They were awfully happy as the whale
saved the day, and thanked Victor
kindly, as they put their sails away.

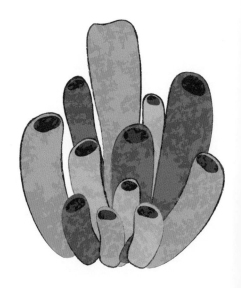

Promising to take care of the ocean and every
creature,
Just like Victor had taught them, as a wise old
teacher.

From that day on, no trawling nets were laid,
They cared for the ocean and a new path was
paved.

Together, they worked hard to keep the ocean clean,
To be in harmony with nature, as we are on the same
team.

5
CHANGES
YOU CAN
MAKE

1: Eat sustainably pole caught fish

2: Eat more plant-based food rather than seafood

3: Use less plastic in your daily life

4: Be kind to all living creatures

5: Join a local clean up by a canal, river or beach such
as UOCEAN® 2050

The End

Printed in Great Britain
by Amazon

18260603R00016